W9-BKQ-824

Dear Parents:

Congratulations! Your child is taking the first steps on an exciting journey. The destination? Independent reading!

STEP INTO READING® will help your child get there. The program offers five steps to reading success. Each step includes fun stories and colorful art or photographs. In addition to original fiction and books with favorite characters, there are Step into Reading Non-Fiction Readers, Phonics Readers and Boxed Sets, Sticker Readers, and Comic Readers—a complete literacy program with something to interest every child.

Learning to Read, Step by Step!

Ready to Read   Preschool–Kindergarten
• big type and easy words • rhyme and rhythm • picture clues
For children who know the alphabet and are eager to begin reading.

Reading with Help   Preschool–Grade 1
• basic vocabulary • short sentences • simple stories
For children who recognize familiar words and sound out new words with help.

Reading on Your Own   Grades 1–3
• engaging characters • easy-to-follow plots • popular topics
For children who are ready to read on their own.

Reading Paragraphs   Grades 2–3
• challenging vocabulary • short paragraphs • exciting stories
For newly independent readers who read simple sentences with confidence.

Ready for Chapters   Grades 2–4
• chapters • longer paragraphs • full-color art
For children who want to take the plunge into chapter books but still like colorful pictures.

STEP INTO READING® is designed to give every child a successful reading experience. The grade levels are only guides; children will progress through the steps at their own speed, developing confidence in their reading.

Remember, a lifetime love of reading starts with a single step!

Step into Reading, Random House, and the Random House colophon are registered trademarks of Penguin Random House LLC.

Visit us on the Web!
StepIntoReading.com
randomhousekids.com

Educators and librarians, for a variety of teaching tools, visit us at RHTeachersLibrarians.com

ISBN 978-0-7364-3662-5 (trade) — ISBN 978-0-7364-8190-8 (lib. bdg.)
ISBN 978-0-7364-3663-2 (ebook)

Printed in the United States of America   10 9 8 7 6 5 4 3 2

Disney
PRINCESS

A Cake to Bake

by Apple Jordan

illustrated by Fabio Laguna & Andrea Cagol

Random House ☖ New York

Princess Tiana loves
to cook.
But she loves
to bake even more!
She bakes brownies
and pies.

Merida is baking cookies.
Who will help her
gather eggs?

"Not me!" say her
brothers.
They are too busy
playing.

The cookies are done!
Who will help
eat them?

"Me! Me! Me!"
say the brothers.

There is a pie contest
at the fair.

Rapunzel is going to
enter her best pie!

PIE
CONTEST

She picks apples.

She makes a tasty crust.

There are so many pies
at the fair.
They all taste yummy!

Rapunzel's pie
is the best.

She wins a blue ribbon!

It is Eric's
birthday.
Ariel wants to
bake him a cake.

She has never
baked before.
The chef is too busy
to help.

Sebastian will help.

Scuttle will help, too.

Sebastian cracks the eggs.

Scuttle pours the milk.

Ariel mixes.

Ariel bakes!

Ariel decorates the cake.
What a mess!

Yum!

The cake tastes great.

Eric knows it was

made with love.

The Beast is sad.
Belle wants
to cheer him up.
She will make him
a special dessert!

Belle looks
in her cookbook.
Brownies would
be perfect!

Belle melts chocolate
and butter.
She mixes in
flour, sugar,
and eggs.

Belle bakes the brownies
in the oven.

The Beast is surprised!
He is happy to have
a sweet friend
like Belle.